Eddie's Toolbox

and How to Make and Mend Things

Sarah Garland

F

FRANCES LINCOLN
CHILDREN'S BOOKS

First published in Great Britain in 2010 and in the USA in 2011 by
Frances Lincoln Children's Books, 4 Torriano Mews,
Torriano Avenue, London NW5 2RZ
www.franceslincoln.com

A catalogue record for this book is available from the British Library.

ISBN 978-1-84780-053-4

Illustrated with watercolours

Printed in Singapore by Tien Wah Press (Pte) Ltd in June 2010
9 8 7 6 5 4 3 2 1

"Quick Mum! Come and look!" called Eddie.

A van had arrived next door. Behind the van was a battered old car.

"Our new neighbours!" said Mum.

A man with curly hair, and a little girl, got out of the car. Lily jumped up and down.

"A friend for me!" she said.

Eddie looked to see whether there was a friend for him too, but there wasn't.

"I'm going to make some welcoming cup cakes," said Mum.

"Me too," said Lily.

When the cup cakes were ready, they went next door and introduced themselves.

"And I am Tom, and this is Tilly," said the man with curly hair.

Lily looked at Tilly.
"Snails?" she said.
"Yes," said Tilly.
Lily and Tilly went down the garden to make a snail collection.

"I need to make things for our new house. Do you like making things Eddie?" asked Tom.
"Sometimes," said Eddie.
"I'm going to start with Tilly's bed," said Tom.

When Mum went home, Eddie decided to stay and watch Tom. Soon Tom needed some help, measuring.

They measured wood for the bed, and Eddie marked the wood with a pencil.

"Will you help me saw it?" asked Tom.

"All right," said Eddie.

So Eddie had a go at sawing. The saw got stuck at first, but Tom soon showed him how to do it.

"Lily! Lily! Bath-time!" called Mum from next door.

Tom lifted Lily over the fence, and she screamed and kicked.

"Lily hates baths," said Eddie.

Suddenly an idea came into his head.

"I could make a boat for Lily out of that old wood," said Eddie.

"That would cheer her up," said Tom.

So Eddie got a rectangle of wood, and put a square piece on top, and a round piece on top of that, and Tom said, “Look in my toolbox and find a hammer and a good long nail.”

So Eddie did that.

When he hit the nail, it bent at first, but Tom showed him how to do it, and soon Eddie hit the nail in straight.

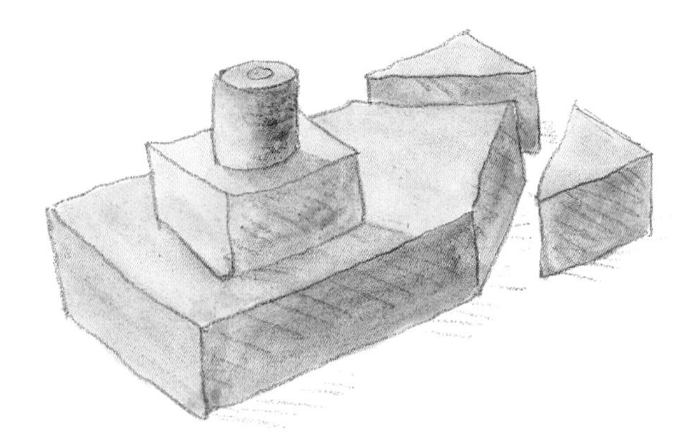

Then Eddie sawed two triangles off the front, and it was like a real boat.

"Thanks, Tom," said Eddie, and he ran back into his own house, and up the stairs to the bathroom. There he found Mum struggling, and Lily in the bath yelling, and water all over the floor.

"Look, Lily!" said Eddie.

"Wow! A boat for me!" cried Lily.

"Fantastic!" said Mum.

And Lily stopped yelling and began to smile, and she played with the boat, and she let Mum wash her.

But she didn't let Mum wash her hair.

The next morning Tom looked over the fence.

"Fancy giving me a hand, Eddie?" he asked.

"Okay," said Eddie.

They worked together, putting up a shelf in the kitchen. Then Tom showed Eddie how to screw hooks in the shelf, and Eddie did that while Tom got on with other things.

When they had finished, Eddie looked at the left-over hooks, and thought hard, until suddenly an idea came into his head.

He found a piece of wood and screwed three hooks into it.

"That looks interesting," said Tom.

"I'm going to fix this high up on the wall in our house, so I can keep my most precious things safe from Lily," said Eddie.

"Lunch for everybody in the garden," called Mum from next door.

There was a big pie for lunch, and soon they were all busy eating.

They were so busy that they didn't see Pusskin, who was creeping up on a lunch of his own.

Suddenly Pusskin had a mouthful of feathers!

"DROP IT, PUSSKIN!" shouted Eddie.

Pusskin dropped the sparrow, but too late. The sparrow was dead!

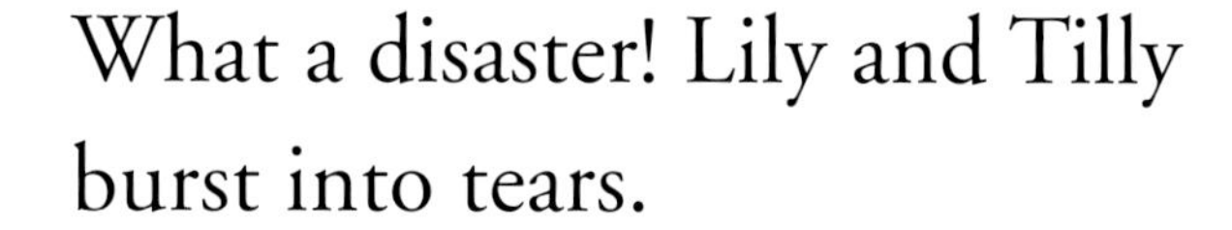

What a disaster! Lily and Tilly burst into tears.

Eddie held the little bird and felt sad.

Mum dug a grave and Tom made a gravestone.
Lily and Tilly picked flowers to put on the grave,
which made them feel better.

Eddie made a little bed for the sparrow to be
buried in, then he thought hard,
until an idea came into his head.

When the sparrow had been buried, Eddie said, "Tom, will you help me make a bird table so the birds in our garden can be safe from cats while they are eating?"

"That's such a good idea," said Tom. "Let's begin at once."

Eddie drew a bird table. It had a long pole so cats couldn't climb it, and a flat bit for bird food, and hooks to hang bird feeders from.

They went into Tom's house and looked for a long pole.

"This is long," said Eddie.

"Well, a bird table is more important than curtains," said Tom.

Then they looked for something flat.

"This is flat," said Eddie.

"Well, a bird table is more important than a tray," said Tom. "Fetch the saw, Eddie."

Eddie sawed the pole to the right length.
"And shall I stick the tray to the pole with a big nail?" asked Eddie.
"Just the job," said Tom.
So Eddie banged in the nail, which went in quite straight, and he screwed in two hooks, and the job was done.

They went back round to Eddie's garden. Mum had a good idea about where the bird table should go.

"Let's put it near the window so we can watch the birds, but not so close that we frighten them," she said.

Everybody helped to dig a hole for the bird table, then they all collected stones to put around the pole to make it steady and strong.

Mum and Tom banged the stones down hard, and covered them with earth and grass.

“Now for the bird food,” said Mum.
She made some bird cakes
with raisins and grated cheese,
mixed with fat.

Eddie put the bird cakes
and some peanuts into
bird feeders.

And he put out a bowl
of water for birds to
drink.

“Snails for birds!” said Lily.

She went with Tilly to fetch their snail collection. But the snails had all escaped, and their home had filled with rainwater.

“Birds like baths,” said Lily thoughtfully.

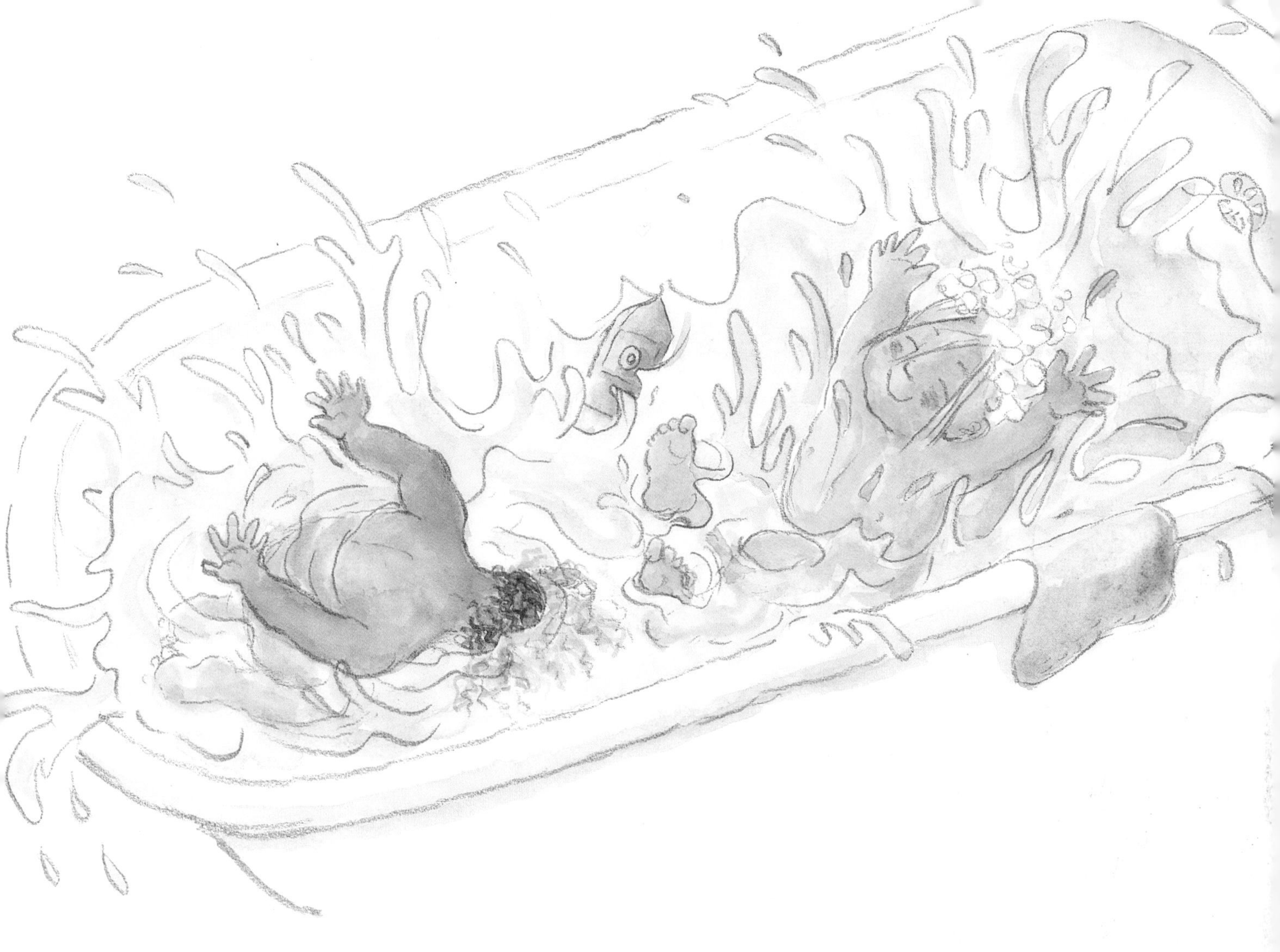

"Bathtime!" called Mum.

"Wash hair!" shouted Lily and Tilly, and they ran inside, and upstairs, and took off their clothes, and jumped straight into the bath.

"Don't drink the bathwater!" cried Mum.

"Birds do," said Lily.

"But you are not a bird," said Mum.

"WE ARE! WE ARE BIRDS!" said Lily and Tilly, and they splashed their arms like wings, and put their heads right in the water, and Mum washed Lily's hair, and Lily didn't mind at all.

Eddie woke up early next morning. He went quietly downstairs to look at the bird table, and was amazed!

There were birds everywhere!
Eating and drinking, and squabbling,
and swinging on the feeder,
and flying back and forth with their
beaks full of food.

Then Mum came down with Lily,
and Tom came round with Tilly,
and they all watched the birds together.

"It's perfect, Eddie," said Mum.

A month passed. Eddie learned a lot about making and mending things.

He glued Tilly's cup together after it got broken.

He sewed Lily's dolly's arm back on after it had an accident.

He tightened the nut on his scooter wheel with Tom's spanner.

He mended Mum's reading glasses
with a tiny screwdriver.

He made an angel
for Tilly's bed,

and an angel for
Lily's bed.

And then, one day, Tom came round with a parcel.

"This is a present for you, Eddie," said Tom. "From your mum and me."

Eddie opened the parcel. He couldn't believe his eyes! It was a beautiful shiny toolbox of his own.

In it there were things for sewing and measuring, and tools for screwing and banging and sawing – everything he needed for making and mending.

"Thanks, Tom. Thanks, Mum," he said. "What shall we make next?"

"Well," said Tom, "your mum says we can make a door in the fence between our gardens. What do you think of that?"

"Great idea!" said Eddie.

He picked up his tool box. "Let's go!" he said.

And everybody helped.

Eddie's tools

Using sharp tools requires patience and common sense.
Be sure that the child is calm and focussed before using a tool,
and that he or she has a clear idea of the result they are aiming for.
Keep the project simple. All tools need to be used with the help of an adult.

Saw

A small tenon saw or handsaw is ideal for a child. One with fine teeth is the easiest to control. Show the child how to hold the saw, with three fingers curled round the handle and the forefinger outstretched to guide the cut. This grip is called the "Three and One". Hold the wood steady for them, or secure it with a cramp or vice. The child should begin to saw very gently, letting the weight of the saw start the cut. If cutting to a marked line, it is best to saw just to the side, so as not to obliterate the line.

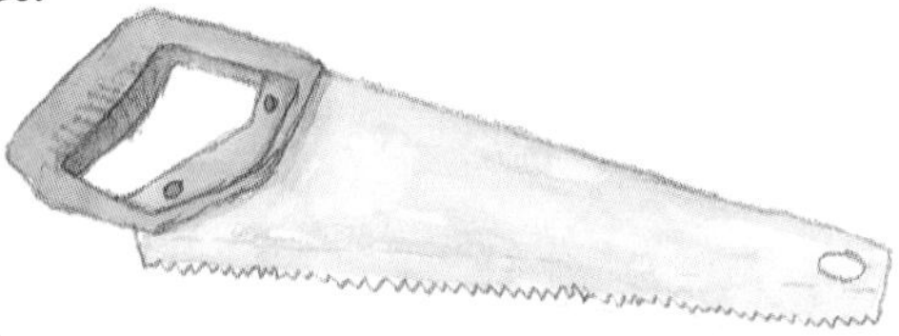

Hammer

Many children will be familiar with the baby game of hammering pegs into holes. Now they can use a hammer with a metal head for banging in metal nails, or a wooden mallet for knocking in wooden pegs or knocking joints together – metal to metal, wood to wood. It is a good idea to drill a small preparatory hole in the wood first. This helps secure the nail so it can be driven home by the child more easily, and also more safely, and it makes it less likely that the wood will split. The child should begin by using the hammer slowly and gently, making little taps. When the nail is well secured, it can be hit harder. It takes some practice to drive a nail in straight and true.

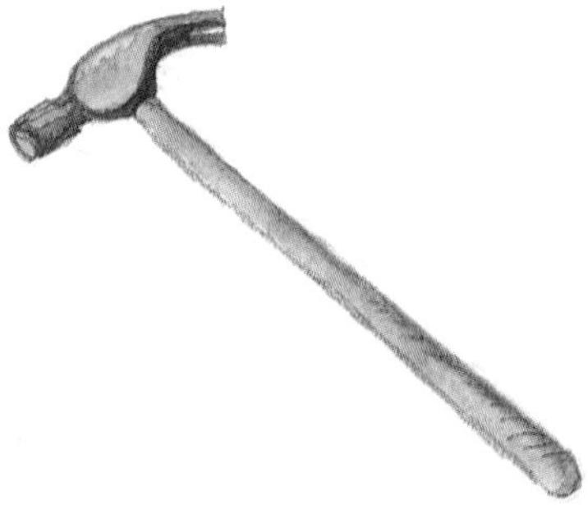

Screwdriver

Again, it is a good idea for the adult to drill a small hole in preparation for the screw, to make using the screwdriver easier and safer. Choose a screwdriver with a head to match the screw head.

Sandpaper

There are different grades of sandpaper, from coarse to fine. If the surface to be sandpapered is very rough, begin with a coarse grade and finish it off with a finer one, working with the grain. Wrap it round a small block of wood to make it easy for a child's hand to hold.

Tape measure or rule

This is a tool that is used for almost every job. You can buy a small tape measure that clips to a pocket or belt.

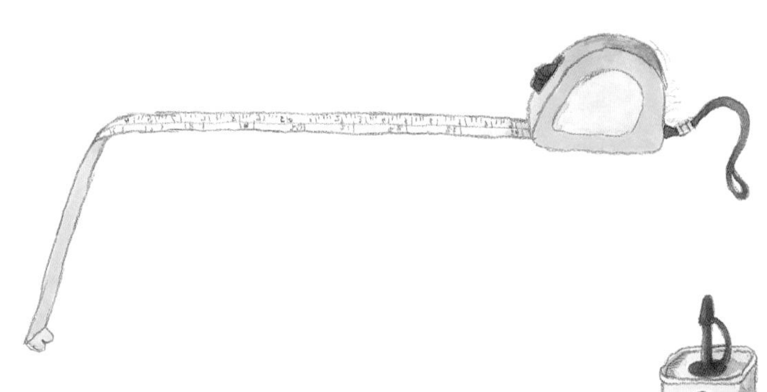

Oil

Buy a container that dispenses a drop of oil at a time, and keep a rag handy.

Glue

Use water soluble glue so that the excess can be washed off hands and clothes with water.

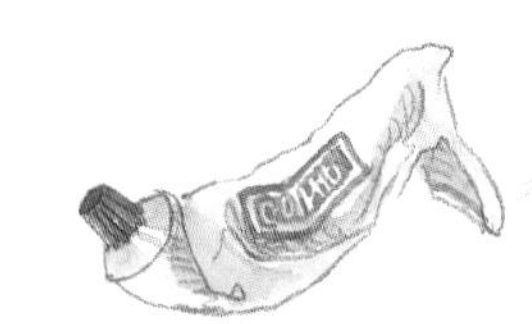

Use a G-cramp or vice, or a heavy weight, to hold the glued surfaces together until the glue is dry and tight.

Read instructions on the container carefully.

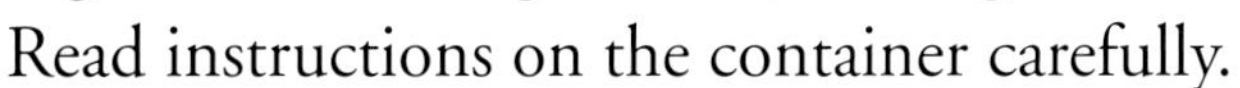

Sewing things

Choose a box in which will fit a small pair of scissors (round-bladed for younger children), some coloured cotton thread, and a packet of needles with good, big eyes.

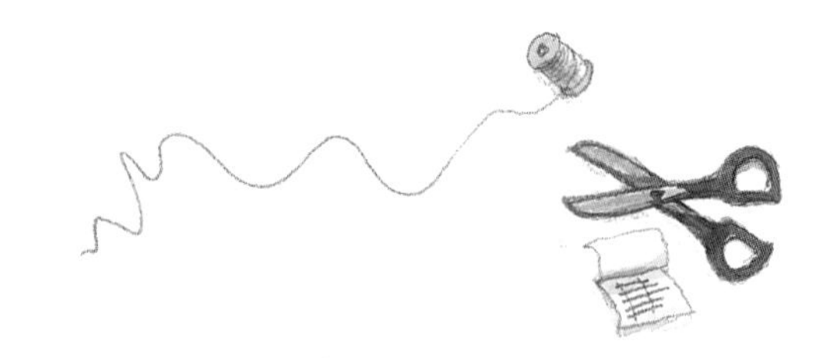

Looking after tools

Keep the toolbox in order, so you always know where tools are. If tools become wet, dry with a rag, then wipe with an oily rag to protect them from rust.

Wood

Apart from being free, one of the advantages of using recycled wood is that it will probably be completely dry. Also, a dismantled piece of furniture or discarded drawer or shelf may be more likely to set the imagination going than a new plank. Watch out for nails!
Hard woods, like oak, are more expensive to buy than soft woods like pine.
They take longer to grow, and tend to have a finer grain.

SAFETY

This is mainly a matter of common sense, but here are some suggestions.
Keep guards on sharp tools, and encourage the child to put them away when they are finished with.
Clean up as you go, and keep the work-space clear to avoid accidents.
Wear shoes – feet are vulnerable in sandals.
Tie up long hair before using tools.
If necessary, use gloves to protect hands and goggles to protect eyes, and a mask if dealing with dust or vapour.
Read safety instructions carefully on all packets and tins before using them.

Eddie's bird table

Looking after birds.

Don't be disappointed if it takes a few days for birds to discover their new bird table. They soon will!

Once begun, it is best to continue to feed birds regularly, even if it is just from a peanut feeder. Small birds, expecting food, will waste precious energy flying to an empty bird table. Food for the table can include bird seed mixtures of sunflower seeds, flaked maize, millet, and chopped (not whole) peanuts. Bread and cake crumbs are good, and dry (not cooked) porridge oats. Don't put out salty, dehydrated or mouldy food.

Whole peanuts go in a bird feeder; bird cakes or suet balls need a larger feeder. Eddie's mum made her cakes by melting lard and stirring in a mixture of dried fruit, grated cheese, bread and cake crumbs, oatmeal and bird seeds – one third lard to two thirds mixture. Leave this to cool, then form into balls – a very sticky procedure!

A shallow bowl of water for birds to drink, especially during dry or frosty weather, is important.

Birds also need to bathe throughout the year, to keep their feathers in good condition.

Finally, there is the garden itself. Shrubby corners and ivy-covered walls are good for nesting and roosting. Berry bearing plants, hedges of native species, and flowers and grasses that have gone to seed are good for food. Blossoming plants and weeds and a pond, however small it is, will attract insects and bugs to eat. Soon you will have a flourishing habitat for birds.

If you only have room for a flower pot or two, or a windowbox, grow a sunflower and for weeks in late summer the flowerheads will be a feeding ground for small birds.